THE ANGEL KNEW PAPA AND THE DOG

THE ANGEL KNEW PAPA AND THE DOG

DOUGLAS KAINE McKELVEY

PHILOMEL BOOKS NEW YORK

Verse on page 7 taken from "Night,"
Songs of Innocence by William Blake.

Editor: Patricia Lee Gauch

Book design by Patrick Collins
The text is set in Sabon.

Library of Congress Cataloging-in-Publication Data
McKelvey, Douglas Kaine.   The angel knew papa and the dog /
Douglas Kaine McKelvey.   p.   cm.
Summary: A seven-year-old girl befriends a large stray dog,
survives a flood that separates her from her beloved father,
and sees an angel.
[1. Fathers and daughters—Fiction.   2. Floods—Fiction.
3. Dogs—Fiction.   4. Angels—Fiction.]   I. Title.
PZ7.M4786744An   1996   [Fic]—dc20   95-47986 CIP AC
IBSN 0-399-23042-4

10 9 8 7 6 5 4 3 2 1

First Impression

For Mansi,
sweetest of all sweet things

PROLOGUE

Papa said that even when I was little I was always shy around strangers and never liked to tell my name to anybody that I didn't already know was my friend.

Some people thought I was a "peculiar" child because of that, but Papa said it wasn't true. He told me that my ways of thinking and seeing and doing things different from other people were just a special part of who I was.

I say that right at the beginning because some folks have heard the story I am about to tell about the angel and Papa and the dog and have not believed it. I can tell by the way they look at me afterward that they think I am very peculiar. But I'm not.

My story, just like my name, is a special part of who I am.

Chapter 1

THE OLD DOG came to us at the end of the
winter when Papa was thirty-six years old
and I was six and a half.

I saw the angel when I was seven.

We lived in a log house together, Papa and I,
that he built with his own hands the year before I was born, which was also the year before Mama died.

Papa built the house in a high corner of a
sloping field, just at the edge of the woods,
where the tall green trees kept it always
shaded from the sun. Sometimes in winter, ice

gathered in the branches of the trees, and Papa said they looked like curious old men with long white beards, milling around our house.

Across the field from our house ran a swift, shallow river that bubbled quietly over the stones in its path. If you sat beside the river, which we often did, it made sounds like a hundred people murmuring words you could almost understand. Papa said the river flowed along as gentle and serene as lambs on clouds, and that was true. Except for one time when it rained for weeks and the river flooded its banks and raged over the field and swallowed our house. But I won't tell you about that until after I tell you about the dog.

Every spring Papa planted a garden close to the river so we wouldn't have to walk very far with our buckets to get water. He would pay our neighbor, Mr. Craven, twenty-five cents to borrow his plow mules, whose names were Bartholomew and Thaddeus Frisco, and we would keep them for a whole day. Mr. Craven lived three miles away over the hills and Papa and me had to wake hours before daylight and walk over together in the cold starlight so we could fetch the mules and bring them back to our field and have them harnessed up and ready to pull the plow by daybreak.

Papa always let me ride home on Thaddeus Frisco's back. Bartholomew was a cantankerous, spiteful old mule, given to ill-tempered fits, stubborn spells, and an occasional bite, but Thaddeus Frisco was as warm and fuzzy and likable as a mule could be. When I rode on his back, as sleepy as I was, I imagined I was on a long caravan journey through some foreign land, but Papa said

I looked so much like a fairy princess that he expected to see a hundred tiny little people flitting through the woods around me.

When Papa plowed or worked in the field, I would make his lunch and carry it out to him. When he came to the end of a row of plants he would lay down his tools and lift me up on his shoulders and we'd walk down to the river to eat.

Sometimes Papa would read to me after we ate if he didn't have too much work to do that day. Papa's voice was deep and soft and steady and low, and it wrapped around me like his arms when he held me, and made me feel safe. Sometimes Papa's voice was like Papa's shoulders because you could ride on it and it would carry you to the river, or to an ancient palace, or to the stars, or to wherever he was reading or speaking about—even back in time to when my mama, whom I never knew, was still alive.

We didn't have many books. When Papa read to me he usually read from the Bible or from a book of poetry. I always liked the story about Balaam's donkey because I could picture how old Bartholomew would like to sass Papa and me if the angel of the Lord would ever open his mouth, but my favorite Bible story was about Noah and the ark, and my favorite poem was by a man named William, who wrote:

> . . . Farewell green fields and happy
>   groves
> Where flocks have took delight.
> Where lambs have nibbled, silent
>   moves
> The feet of angels bright . . .

That was my favorite poem even before I saw the angel.

CHAPTER 2

SOME PEOPLE WHERE WE LIVED liked to mark the start of spring strictly by the numbers on the calendar, or by the moon, or by the opening of the earliest flowers. For me it was the arrival of the heavy thunderstorms every year that always tied the tail of winter to the nose of spring.

One late March afternoon, Papa was reading to me by the river when we noticed a line of dark clouds pouring in fast and low from the west. The clouds seemed to tumble and roll like water boiling over the rim of a kettle. It was the kind of clouds we would ever afterward call "serpent clouds."

Papa's brow furrowed as he took a long look at the sky. It wasn't often that Papa was surprised by anything that happened in the open spaces of the river and woods. Over the years he had learned something of the ways of the weather and of the river and of the coos and crows and chitterings of animals and insects. To him, everything was filled with a music. The feel of the air and the look of the clouds and the sound of the crickets all came together like violins and flutes and cellos playing different parts of a melody, and if you studied on it long enough, he claimed, you could usually make out what tune they were warming up to play.

But not always. When the night of the flood eventually came, even Papa was caught unawares. I'll tell you about that later though, after I finish telling about the dog.

Papa scanned the clouds that afternoon in March and then closed the book in his lap and told me to run on ahead to the house to latch the wooden shutters and light some candles. "Something doesn't feel right," he said. I ran off along the little path through the field while Papa hurried up the hill toward the garden to gather in our early planting tools and seed pouches. We always planted a stand of cabbages together, Papa and I, long before the other crops.

I was halfway up the little path when the storm suddenly knocked the breath out of the sky so that the wind dropped quickly and rushed through the forest with a deep hiss. The tall green trees began to whip and twist like frenzied, chained men trying to free themselves. I had never seen our woods so angry.

Near the edge of the clearing I paused to look over my shoulder, hoping Papa was close behind. It was there that the underbrush exploded in my face.

A snarling, black shape burst from the tall thicket of grass and drove hard into my chest, forcing me backward and knocking me flat to the ground. I found myself pinned down with a paw on each shoulder, staring into the face of a big, raggedy beast who was barking and carrying on in a most ferocious manner. I screamed for Papa but he had heard the commotion and was already bolting across the field with his hoe in hand.

"Get away! Get!" Papa hollered, running up at the dog with his hoe raised and ready to strike.

The huge dog bounded off me and moved about ten feet up the path. There he sat down in the dirt and barked again. Papa ran at him a second time, trying to scare him off. "Get away!" he shouted.

But the raggedy dog didn't budge. He just cast Papa a slow sidelong glance and kept right on barking, determined to hold his ground.

I sat up in the dirt and wiped the tears out of my eyes. Raindrops were slapping the ground all around us. I saw Papa edging up close to the dog. The dog's back was twitching, but otherwise he stayed still as a stone. A low, threatening growl rumbled and played in his throat.

Then two strange things happened at once that I'll never forget. A bolt of lightning pierced the low clouds and shattered the top of a huge oak tree not forty feet away with a bang as loud as the inside of a cannon. At that same instant, a sudden shape sprang up like a firecracker flashing in the grass, and Papa and the dog both leapt back and away from it.

I could see Papa silhouetted against the crackling, glowing oak tree. He raised the hoe over his head and brought it down with all his strength, one, two, three times, while the dog skitted around his feet, barking.

Papa wiped the rainwater off his brow with the back of his hand and let the hoe drop to the ground. A long, twisted shadow now lay at his feet. Papa looked up at the tree. The old oak was still smoldering. Papa turned and looked at me for a long time before he came and sat down.

"That old puppy didn't mean to scare you," he finally said. "He was just watching over you." Papa paused to catch his breath and I saw a little mist in his eyes. "There was a serpent, coiled in the grass beside the path. If you had taken another seven steps you would have stepped right on it. That big dog knocked you over to keep you from getting bit."

The dog was still barking at the torn body of the serpent in the mud: Papa called to him and he gave one more bark and ambled over to us. He sat down in a puddle and licked my face.

The dog's paws were the biggest I'd ever seen. "Papa, his feet look like lion's feet," I said.

Papa speculated maybe that was why the dog had been so brave. His lion feet gave him lion courage.

When we got inside the house, it had all but quit raining. Papa said it was one of those storms that hollers loud and runs fast. We pulled our beds up close to the fireplace and sat down to eat bowls of hot potato soup while we dried out. The dog came in and curled up on the floor next to our feet.

After I had finished eating, Papa let me feed the dog with my leftovers. He lapped the soup up slowly like he was some gentleman eating at a fancy dinner. It made Papa and me laugh.

"He's got more table manners than the both of us put together!" Papa said.

When the dog was finally satisfied that he had hunted down the last drop in the bowl, he raised his head and gave my foot a friendly lick. Then he lay back down with a long stretch of his legs, pushing his big paws out toward the fire's warmth.

After we cleaned up the kettle and bowls, Papa sang some of the old hymns that he and Mama used to sing together. His voice filled the room with a full and quiet sweetness, like the lapping of the river along its banks, and I curled up under the covers and tried to stay awake and listen as long as I could.

Nothing bad would ever happen to me as long as Papa and I were together, I thought. His voice was so gentle and good and strong that certainly no evil thing could ever reach through it to take me. I turned my back to the fire and closed my eyes.

While Papa sang, the old dog snored lightly beside my bed, occasionally stirring to thump his tail appreciatively on the wooden floor.

"Well, Mary," I heard Papa sigh when he must have thought I was already asleep, "it was a close one today."

Mary was my mother's given name.

CHAPTER 3

THE DOG STAYED WITH US off and on for almost a year after that, up until the time of the next big storm, when the river rose to flood. He'd leave for three or four days sometimes, but never did very many mornings pass before he'd show up back on the porch again, waiting for us to open the door. I decided he must be a famous dog explorer, who went off in search of adventures and treasures. I think that's why we ended up naming him Lewis and Clark—in honor of the brave explorers who had mapped out the western territories for President Jefferson.

Papa said that Lewis and Clark was the kind of dog that wasn't good for much except to save your life once in a while. Most of the time he slept in the shade under the porch stoop or chased through the woods after rabbits and squirrels. A couple of times he even followed rabbits right through the rows of Papa's corn, sending stalks crashing and flying like he was some crazed lumberjack. But whenever I crossed the field to take Papa his lunch, Lewis and Clark would gallop out from wherever he was and walk close beside me like he was guarding the Queen of England, and Papa couldn't help but love him for the way he looked after me.

One hot day in August Lewis and Clark turned up after one of his long holidays and Papa decided it was as good a reason as any to come in early from the field and sit up on the porch drinking lemonade from a jar we'd chilled in the river.

We read the Genesis story of Jacob's wrestling match with the angel, and I asked Papa if he had ever seen an angel with his own eyes and he took a sip of the lemonade and furrowed his brow and thought on it for a while and then he said he couldn't say yes and then again he couldn't say no, on account of angels didn't always come down with wings and flaming swords and announce themselves.

"You'd probly have to be about three parts hound dog," he said, patting Lewis and Clark on the head, "to sniff out a real angel."

What Papa said might be true most of the time, but I knew at once it was an angel when I saw the light glowing on the floodwaters that winter, and I made it a point to tell Papa so afterward.

CHAPTER 4

THE DRIZZLY WINTER RAINS started in late November that year, just after Thanksgiving, in the early days of the "cozy season" that always stretched into late February when Papa would again begin the yearly cycle of plowing, planting, and harvesting.

In the meantime, we had many hours to spend holed up by a warm fire reading books together, or gathering walnuts in the forest, or planning our Christmas surprises. Without the garden to tend to, we could usually finish our chores by noon and spend our afternoons as we saw fit.

One day we went into town to buy a few things and to see if we could sell our modest surplus crop. A retired schoolteacher offered us a stack of old books in trade for our pumpkins and squash. We accepted them quicker than cash. When we got home we scattered the books across the bed and sorted through them like they were pirate's treasure. There were seven books in all: *Paradise Lost, Robinson Crusoe, Le Morte d'Arthur, Piers Plowman, The Faerie Queen,* Shakespeare's *Hamlet,* and *The Autobiography of Benjamin Franklin.*

We deliberated a while over what to read first, but Papa finally told me they were all good and just to close my eyes and pick one. I picked *Piers Plowman.*

It was the coziest feeling in the world, lying on my bed in front of the fire that evening with all those books around me, listening to Papa's gentle voice and sipping hot vegetable broth.

Papa lit his pipe as he read, and the burning tobacco smoke slowly filled the room with that sweet aroma Papa liked to call "southern incense." I hoped we would get snowed in for a week. The only thing missing from our cheery little house was Lewis and Clark. He had been away for almost two days. "I hope he's somewhere warm," I told Papa.

> In a summer season when the sun
> was mild
> I got myself up into a garb as
> though I'd grown into a sheep . . .

The words of *Piers Plowman* danced from Papa's tongue, sifting around the room like dandelion tufts riding on the wind.

> . . . I went wide in the world,
> watching for wonders.
> And on a May morning on
> Malvern Hills

A marvel befell me—magic it
seemed . . .

The rain started as a patter just after dusk that
evening and came on steadily through the
night. Occasionally clouds broke over the forest, allowing patches of moonlight to crawl
through the window and across my bedcov-
ers, but the rains soon returned and the moonlight would fade again. As the night wore on,
Papa and I sometimes stirred in our beds
when we heard the tiny clink of sleet tapping
on our windowpane. The sounds of the cold
wet night outside, we both agreed, made our
cozy room feel just like a warm little nest.

When the freezing rains had gone on for
two whole days, Papa bundled up and walked
down to the river. He came back saying that
the field was a garden of ice and that a band
of Eskimos was camped out there roasting a

penguin on a spit. Papa never lost his imagination.

We read *The Faerie Queene* and the first fifty pages of *Paradise Lost,* and still the rains poured down. After five days, the weather finally broke and the downpour slacked off to a fine mist, and Papa and I decided to wander out for a look. The sky was pitched above us like a low, wide tent, all eerie and pale. It was the first time I ever remembered not hearing the songs of birds in the trees around our house.

Everything was grey, and cold, and still. We marched up into the wood a little ways and turned around. The forest was too lonely with nothing stirring and only the crunching of our own footsteps to greet our ears. It was better to be back inside, drinking cider by the fire.

Sometime during that night, the rains

started up again in earnest. We woke the next morning to a wet, dismal world and stirred our oatmeal in silence. Neither of us felt like reading anymore. Papa cleaned and sharpened all his gardening tools, while I took pieces of an old sheet and tried to stitch together doll clothes.

"What if Lewis and Clark is lost out there somewhere?" I asked Papa, looking over the windowsill into the woods.

"Old Lewis has a compass for a brain," Papa replied with a chuckle. "I expect he's about as lost out there as a pig in a pie plate."

Three days later the rain was still settled in and there was still no sign of Lewis and Clark. I quit counting after that.

CHAPTER 5

THE RIVER ITSELF wasn't what was mostly to
blame for the flood, Papa told me later. The
real culprit was the blanket of ice on the roads
and forests and fields that kept all the water
from draining off. Rainwater was pouring
into the river from the hills up in the forest,
channeled down from gentle slopes a mile or
more away. Even twenty miles upriver the
water was steadily rising into a wall that
would wind like a serpent through the bends
of the long valley and coil around us as we
slept.

Not even Papa could have known.

One morning we stepped shivering onto the porch and watched the river coursing through our front yard. It had appeared overnight, but now it flowed along as nonchalantly as if it had always been there. I picked up a stick and knocked long icicles from the edge of the roof. Papa drug out his cane fishing pole and dropped the line over the porch rail into the water to make me laugh. "I guess we won't have to carry our watering buckets to the garden anymore," he said.

"We might have to hold our breath to pick our peas and corn, though," I giggled.

I was worried about the floodwaters at first, but Papa didn't expect that the river could rise more than another foot, if that much.

"But if it did get too high someone could come get us in a boat, couldn't they?" I asked.

"Well," Papa answered, "I doubt if anyone on this shallow stretch of river owns a boat. But you don't need to worry. We'll be fine."

Early that afternoon we had surprise visitors. Our old mule friends, cantankerous Bartholomew and gentle Thaddeus Frisco, came wandering down through the trees behind our house and pressed themselves flat up against it, trying to get out of the rain. They were a sad sight with their heads down and water dripping from the ends of their noses. I snatched a corncob to lure them through the water up onto the porch, and Papa tied their tethers to the railing. We threw old blankets over them to warm them up.

"Why did Bartholomew and Thaddeus walk all the way over here in the rain?" I asked.

Papa didn't know.

"We'll go see Mr. Craven when the rain lets up, though," he said, "just to make sure he's alright."

Mr. Craven, we found out later, was already lying on a cot in a makeshift shelter with three other families, five miles upriver. His house had been flooded, and his shed had been uprooted and carried off by the swollen water. He was lucky it had happened in daylight so he could at least see to find his way out through the forest.

Just before he abandoned his house, Mr. Craven had shooed Bartholomew and Thaddeus out of their pen, hoping they would take to some sheltered high ground further up in the timber. For whatever reason, the mules had come roundabout instead through the wet, frozen wood to our place.

The flood had been deceptive. Papa and I were completely trapped. In the short hours it had taken the mules to find us, the waters had risen close to another half a foot. We were completely cut off from everyone up-river who knew us, and we didn't even know it yet.

CHAPTER 6

STANDING ON THE PORCH with the mules that evening, I couldn't help but wonder how Noah might have felt on the day the big rains began as he took one long, last look around at the world that was about to be destroyed by the great Flood. How strange and wonderful it all must have seemed when he didn't know if he would ever see it again.

I could almost picture how when God was reaching down and closing the door of the ark, Noah might have been in there standing on tiptoe trying to see out for as long as he could. The Bible says Noah was six hundred years old when he went into the ark. I bet he noticed things in that last minute that he hadn't paid any attention at all to for the last five hundred fifty years.

I looked around through the rain to see what I would notice if I were Noah climbing into the ark. At first I could only hear the wind whispering like bird wings in the trees. Then I saw the moon low in the sky, round and wide as the eye of a cat. As I looked at it through the swaying branches, I could all but imagine that it had blinked. I walked to the side of the porch. There, in the dusky light, the wooded hills around us seemed to sweep out and upward like the waves of a deep green ocean.

It was a world of wonders, Papa once told me, for anyone who cared to slow down and take a look.

The cold was beginning to make me shiver, so I gave the mules a final pat and turned to go back inside. Beside the doorway I saw a bucket of rich black dirt that Papa had brought up from the field months before so I could plant late flowers around the house. As I passed by it, I scooped up a small handful of the frozen earth and carried it inside with me. Noah, the Bible says, like Papa, was a man of the soil. I'm sure he would have done the same.

Papa had never been too busy to stop and wonder at the lesser things in the earth. He had always noticed things like the roots in the garden, the smooth river stones, and the little black eyes of the field mice. As I felt the cold soil warming in my hand, I remembered how Papa had called me over once when he uncovered a nest of baby moles in the garden. We had picked them up and stroked their soft grey fur while they tickled our hands with their wide front feet. Neither of us said a word. It was a moment blessed by silence, a whole new wonder.

Kind of like seeing an angel, only not as bright.

CHAPTER 7

W<small>E NEVER KNEW</small> if ornery Bartholomew lost
his footing or got spooked or just decided
he'd had enough of standing around on our
porch, but sometime in the night we heard a
strange noise and looked out to see the old
mule in the water, struggling against the current with his rope still tied to the post. The
water had risen rapidly in the darkness, and
now covered even the top step leading up to
the porch. Papa moved fast. He eased out,
grabbed the rope with one hand, and leaned
over the rail trying to loose the rope from the
panicked animal's neck.

Between Papa and Bartholomew and the tug of the current, though, there was too much pressure on the porch rail. It snapped like kindling, and Papa tumbled in. He and Bartholomew were instantly washed away out into the darkness.

"Papa!" I called, "Papa! Papa!"

But all I heard back was the constant rushing of the water hissing past like a witch's broom, and the creaking of the house as the river swelled to push against it.

Papa was gone.

I gathered up candles from the house as fast as I could and set them out on the porch for Papa to see his way home. Huddling against Thaddeus Frisco for warmth, I waited and waited, sobbing all the while until my side ached.

In time I grew so cold that I couldn't feel my feet and fingers anymore. I fumbled to untie Thaddeus' tether and led him inside with me. I left the candle stubs burning on the porch for Papa.

What more could I do?

I crawled up into Papa's bed and burrowed under his covers. I could smell the familiar smells on his pillow—a mixture of earth, and plants, and sweet pipe tobacco, and shaving soap. As I lay there, the house would give an occasional lurch, swaying from side to side like a big, lazy boat. Thaddeus leaned in a corner with his droopy ears to the wall and his gentle eyes closed. It looked for all the world like he was deep in prayer.

I walked across the wooden floor to stand beside him, and together we called out to the Lord on behalf of Papa and Bartholomew, petitioning their safe return.

When I took a step back toward the bed, my foot set down in an icy puddle. Water was seeping up through the floor. I had been so worried about Papa that I hadn't even imagined the river might rise and enter the house. I was so scared that I climbed back into Papa's bed and curled up in a little ball with the pillow pulled over my head. When I finally mustered enough courage to peek out, I could see water spreading slowly over the whole floor.

I cried myself into a trembling, troubled sleep.

Chapter 8

THE LIGHT FROM THE ANGEL wasn't like the light from the boat lantern. The boat lantern, when it appeared, had a flame in the middle that pushed quivering shadows out from the edges. The angel, on the other hand, glowed with brilliant light all around, and cast no shadows. I say this because people tried to tell me afterward that what I saw on that night was not an angel, but a glowing lantern playing tricks on my imagination.

What I saw was an angel.

I opened my eyes in the deep of night and

saw Thaddeus Frisco sloshing around the room, trying to find a haven from the cold water that was now up to his knees. Books, pieces of firewood, and other odd items floated and bobbed around the room like corks in a bucket. The front door was open, and I thought at first that Papa must be back, but it was really only the rising river that had pushed it in. Moonlight reflected off the water, bouncing from the smooth sides of drifting objects. The poor house groaned terribly with the weight of the flood that filled and circled it. I was seized with a sudden fright that we were going to drown and that Papa would never find us but would wander the riverbank for years, calling out our names.

I sat up on the bed and called to Thaddeus. He twitched his big fuzzy ears and slowly waded over to me. I carefully clambered onto his back and whispered to him, trying to soothe both of us. "Now, Thaddeus, I want you to be a very brave mule. We have to leave before the flood comes more. I will hang on to your back, and you will swim us out of the water, and Papa and Bartholomew will be waiting for us over there all safe and dry."

I clenched Thaddeus' mane in my little fists and pointed him toward the door, gently kicking his barreled sides to get him going. He had always been a patient mule, and quick to obey once he understood what was expected of him. Now Thaddeus seemed unsure for a moment, but then he gave a soft little grunt and plodded off through the water as I spoke encouragements into his ear.

He put his head out the doorway and stopped in his tracks. After that, I couldn't get him to put so much as a foot on the submerged porch.

45

"Thaddeus, we must keep going," I said, giving him another gentle poke with my heels. "We must be brave."

Thaddeus still didn't move. He laid his ears back flat against his head. Inside, I heard the far wall of the house give a sharp splitting pop.

"Thaddeus," I pleaded, "we have to leave! Please go!"

But the mule stood stiff as a statue.

"We have to find Papa," I cried in frustration. "We have to swim out away from the house!" I started pulling on poor Thaddeus' mane and kicking him in the sides as hard as I could. I became angry and held on with one fist while I pounded on his back with the other. But Thaddeus didn't flinch. He just turned his face around and looked at me with such a grave, somber expression in his eyes that I stopped my screaming and punching and looked out over the waters for the first time. What I saw made the breath draw up short in my throat.

The angel.

There, just beyond the porch railing, the angel hovered and glowed, wonderful beyond imagining, shedding light far across the water, like stars spilling from the cupped hands of God. I was so startled that I let go of the mane and almost tumbled from Thaddeus' back.

"An angel," I whispered.

The angel was as still as a hundred-year oak, its wings spread far above us in the night, its robes pure white and blinding, its skin like a burning copper flame. The hands of the angel were firm and sure, the face was strong as any river, and the eyes seemed to blaze deeper than all eternity.

I forgot about my plans to swim ashore with Thaddeus. I forgot my fear of drowning

47

and my worry for Papa. I forgot about everything but the angel.

The angel looked into my eyes in a perfect stillness. A stillness without words and a stillness without questions, but a stillness with more meaning than all words that were ever spoken and all questions that were ever asked.

The angel knew me. I knew that.

And the angel knew Papa and the dog.

And the angel knew Thaddeus Frisco and Bartholomew and Mr. Craven and everyone in the whole town.

And the angel knew old Noah, who had weathered a worse flood than ours.

And the angel even knew my mama, who had died before I could remember.

The angel didn't move or breathe a word to tell me any of this. I sat perfectly still and quiet in that light, and I just knew.

And I knew in the same way that no matter what happened to us, even if it was time to close our eyes and take our hand and lead us down through the valley of the shadow of death, where Mama had walked long ago, all was well. The angel was with us.

The angel of the Lord.

CHAPTER 9

WHEN THADDEUS FRISCO gave a long whinny I blinked my eyes and saw that the angel had passed from sight, but something like music still hung in the air around us, echoing and passing across the waters for a long while.

CHAPTER 10

AND THEN, faint but unmistakable, Lewis and Clark barked. The sound was a ways off, but still close enough that I could hear it over the river. I could hardly believe it was true.

"Lewis and Clark!" I shouted. "Lewis and Clark!"

I heard his bark again, somewhere upstream and off to the side. I pulled on Thaddeus' mane so that he backed out of the doorway. This time he obeyed. We maneuvered slowly over to the side window and looked out. My heart leapt! A little boat with a lantern in the middle was moving steadily toward the house, and there, facing me with his paws up on the side of the boat, was Lewis and Clark.

I managed to fish a nearby piece of firewood out of the water. Raising it over my head, I drove it through the window as hard as I could. Glass crashed to the water below.

"Over here!" I yelled out to the boat. "I'm over here!"

"Hang on, honey, we'll be right there," a woman's voice called back over the noise of the flood. Lewis and Clark started up barking again when he heard my voice.

I waited nervously as the boat inched nearer. When they were still a good piece away, though, something seemed to go wrong. The lantern stopped moving toward me and then began to creep slowly back upstream.

"Wait!" I shouted after them. "Don't leave me!"

The woman hollered something back, but her words were lost in the rushing of the water. Even Lewis and Clark's barks were muffled by the noise.

I sat on Thaddeus' back, watching out the window for a long time before I could tell that the light was finally moving toward us again. This time it didn't stop at all, but came straight for the house.

As it drew closer, I could see that the boat was a rowboat turned completely backward with the nose pointed upstream, against the current. A rope was tied to the front of the boat and stretched out over the water toward the trees. The woman was hanging on to the rope and feeding it out a little at a time so that the boat moved along bit by bit toward the house, but wasn't swept sideways or turned over by the current.

It took several minutes for the woman to bring the boat up beneath the window, but then the current pitched and slammed it against the wall constantly so that she couldn't even stand up at all for fear of falling out. She was hanging on to Lewis and Clark with one hand just to keep him from trying to jump to me.

"Okay, honey," she hollered, "you do what I tell you and we'll have you on dry land in a few minutes. Now is there something in there like a rope or a long blanket that you could find and bring back over to the window?"

I squinted my eyes in the dim moonlight. The down mattress from my bed was floating in the middle of the room. I prodded Thaddeus toward it and managed to retrieve a soggy blanket, which we carried back to the window. Poor Thaddeus was shivering awfully from standing belly-deep in the cold all that time.

"Now what I want you to do," she shouted, her voice sounding hoarse from the effort, "is to tie one end of that blanket around your middle good and tight, okay? And then I want you to tie the other end around something in there that's not going to move, like a wooden post or a spike in the wall. Then you can climb out, and we'll get you lowered down into the boat."

I tied the blanket around my waist and looked all around for something to fix the other end to. The only things I could see, though, were the roof beams, which were too high to reach, and the kettle hooks on the distant hearth.

"There's nothing I can tie it to," I hollered out the window. "It won't reach."

The woman thought for a moment.

"There must be something. What are you standing on now?" she asked.

I looked down. "I'm sitting on Thaddeus Frisco."

"You're sitting on what?"

"I'm sitting on Thaddeus Frisco. He's a mule," I yelled down to her. "He belongs to my neighbor."

The woman gave a short laugh and then jerked to catch her balance as the boat knocked against the side of the house. Her lantern pitched over and snuffed out. "Tie the end of the blanket around the mule's neck," she said. "He's not going to go anywhere."

I bound the blanket tight around Thaddeus' neck and eased my feet onto the windowsill.

"But how will Thaddeus get out?" I asked suddenly. "I don't want to leave him in here all by himself!"

"First we're going to worry about getting you safely back to your papa," the woman answered.

"My papa? Have you seen him? Is he okay?" I asked all at once.

"He's waiting for you," was all she shouted up.

I turned back and kissed old Thaddeus on the top of his head and whispered in his ear, "Thaddeus Frisco, do not be afraid. Remember that the angel of the Lord is with you." Thaddeus just blinked his eyes and stood perfectly still for as long as it took me to crawl over the windowsill and lower myself down to the woman, who caught me and pulled me into the little boat. She plopped me down in the bottom like a sack of potatoes while Lewis and Clark licked my face over and over. He was so excited to see me that he wouldn't stop wriggling and whining. His tail pounded hard against the sides of the boat. I wrapped my arms around him.

"You can call me Mary," the woman said with a little smile.

I looked at her closely. She had a sweet, round face and dark, curly hair that trailed down over her shoulders. The moon above cast a soft light on her cheeks.

I was feeling so many things that I couldn't even talk. I could see Mary's arms tremble as she pulled hard on the rope to draw us back to shore, and I was thinking about my mama and my papa, and I could feel the cold wind running through my hair and the water splashing on my face and hands, and I could see the stars scattered here and there through the clouds, and I could feel Lewis and Clark's warm fur against my arms, and I could hear the trees around our house whisper and sigh as the little boat passed between them.

I looked up at the window one last time and saw that it was softly glowing from the inside, and there, outlined by the glow, were the raised ears of Thaddeus Frisco Mule, still patiently waiting.

"Thaddeus," I called after him, "Thaddeus!"

His big ears twitched at the sound of my voice, but he didn't move at all.

"Maybe he'll find his own way out," Mary said hopefully.

And he did. Only it wasn't through the window or the door. Sometime that very night Thaddeus went out through the valley of the shadow, and I know that he went patiently and without fear, for the angel of the Lord was with him.

No one even saw it happen, but the whole house, with good Thaddeus in it, was swept up and carried away and split apart by the flood so that nothing remained of it but the big hearthstones that sank to the bottom, too heavy to move.

CHAPTER 11

WHEN WE FINALLY REACHED the edge of the water, Mary pulled the boat up onto the shore and lifted me out. Lewis and Clark jumped out too, shaking big drops of water and bits of ice from his coat. I followed Mary up the hill a little ways to where a pretty buckskin horse was snorting and stamping its cold hooves on the ground.

"Fletcher's going to take us straight back to your papa," Mary said. She helped me climb up into the saddle and then, grabbing the reins in her left hand, she swung up behind me.

We left the boat up in the woods and rode back to Mary's house as fast as her horse could maneuver over the icy, uneven terrain. Mary relit the lantern and let me sit in front holding it.

We plunged along through the wood. The dark green trees seemed to appear from nowhere, quiver wildly, and fall away as the passing lantern light spun shadows around them. This was a long ride back to Papa, and I waited anxiously.

Lewis and Clark ran ahead so fast that we didn't see him at all once we started off, but on occasion the wind carried his gruff bellowing back to our ears. "He's more than a half mile ahead of us," Mary said.

Mary gracefully guided her little horse along the path with only the slightest tug of her hands on the reins. As we rode, her arms held me in on either side. She sometimes sang quietly as we traveled along, and once when she leaned forward to speak to me, her soft cheek brushed against my ear.

It was in that moment that I first knew how much I had always missed my mama.

I suddenly wanted to tell Mary that Mama had been named Mary too, and that Mama also sang with a beautiful voice, and that someday in heaven Papa said I would finally get to see her. But I was too shy to say anything, and I was still so anxious about Papa.

I must have dozed off sometime later, because the lantern slipped from my hands and fell to the ground with a clatter and a crash. Mary didn't even stop to pick it up. "It's okay, honey," she said gently, "we've got plenty of moonlight to see by."

A few minutes later, Mary leaned over my shoulder and pointed. "There it is up ahead," she said. "See that light through the trees? That's my house. We're almost there."

We came into a little clearing that surrounded Mary's house. It was smaller than mine and Papa's, but even in the dark it was cute and homey as could be with firelight glowing through the window. Mary pulled back on the reins, and the horse stopped near the door. Lewis and Clark was already there, waiting impatiently to be let in.

"I want you to know before you go in that your papa is hurt," Mary said, helping me slide down from the horse, "and I don't know if he'll even be awake."

Something in her voice made me stop and look at her face.

"What's wrong with him?" I asked.

"I don't know," she said. "I'm pretty sure he has some broken bones, but whether there's anything more than that, I couldn't tell."

I looked at Mary quietly for a moment, wondering if she was really telling me everything she knew.

"Is my papa going to die?" I finally asked.

Mary put her hand on my cheek and gave a sad little smile. I thought I could see a tear in her eye.

"I don't know, honey," she said. "I wish I could tell you for certain that he was going to be okay, but I don't know. I don't even know what happened to him."

I knew then that she was telling me the truth.

I nodded my head and she opened the door and I followed her inside. Lewis and Clark for once didn't dash in ahead of me. He lagged at my heels, seeming mournful and unsure.

Mary's house was mostly one big room. She had a table and some chairs and a cupboard and a sleeping loft up above with a feather mattress in it, but other than that there wasn't any furniture. At the far end of the room was a rock fireplace, and there, under a blanket on the floor in front of the fire, I saw my papa lying still as a stone.

I crossed the room to where he was and knelt down beside him. I could see a gash across his right cheek and a deep bruise above his right temple. I looked up at Mary. She was watching him too. It was several long seconds before we finally saw the blanket over his chest rise as he drew in a breath.

I reached out and softly touched his forehead. "Papa?" I said, "Can you hear me?"

He stirred a little but didn't wake.

Mary knelt beside me and put her arm around my shoulders. Lewis and Clark sat by Papa's feet. I felt myself start to sob.

"Papa . . ." I said again. "Oh Papa, please wake up!"

And then he did.

First his brow furrowed ever so slightly, and then, a moment later, he gave a groan.

Papa's eyes blinked open halfway, fluttered, and opened wide.

He looked startled when he saw me and he tried to sit up, but the pain in his body hit him like a snakebite, and he dropped back to the floor with a little gasp.

"Papa!" I said. "Papa, Papa, Papa!" I leaned toward him and stretched my arms around him. I know it must have hurt him dreadfully to move at all, but Papa slowly reached up with his left arm and pulled me closer to him, and we both cried and cried and cried until we could hardly breathe.

"She's safe," he finally whispered. "My little girl is safe."

A few minutes later, Papa lost consciousness again. Mary said that she had seen something like it before and it was probably due to the blow on his head. For the next few hours, we tended him together, adding blankets when he got chilled and taking them off when he was feverish. Whenever he woke up enough, we would try to spoon warm soup into his mouth, but it wasn't easy to do with him flat on his back.

Once when I spilled soup down his cheek, he looked up at me and smiled weakly.

"I think your papa's gonna be alright now that you're here," Mary told me when he had fallen back asleep.

It raised my spirits to hear her say that. I already knew that Mary told the truth.

CHAPTER 12

WHEN PAPA AND I RETURNED to our place to have a look a week and a half later, after he'd had some time to mend, there was nothing but a wide, peaceful lake stretching off through the trees, and Papa remarked that it looked like there had never even been a house or a field or a garden there at all. We sat directly on the ground by the lake and ate the lunches that Mary had packed for us, though I had to help Papa unwrap his on account of his broken right arm and his cracked ribs, which were still so very tender. The bruise over his temple was fading.

Papa had already told me how his injuries had come about on that night when he was first swept off downriver, on the night of the angel.

He said the current would have drowned him in the first two minutes if a tree hadn't of floated up behind and bumped him in the head. Thankfully, he had his wits about him enough to pull himself up onto the tree and lock his arms and legs amongst the branches. He rode that way down the river for several miles until he was almost passed out from the cold.

Papa told me that no person could ever have swum out of that flood no matter how strong they were. He said that if the angel hadn't of been there and if Thaddeus Frisco had done what I wanted and had jumped into the water with me on his back, I would have been swept right off and drowned before I knew it. The angel had come to spare my very life, Papa said.

Papa was the only one who ever believed that it really was an angel.

Except for Mary.

Mary had found Papa on that terrible night, when the river coughed him up half drowned and frozen at the water's edge, not a hundred feet from her house.

The place she lived in was further down the river than I had ever been before that night, at a point where two rivers joined together and the waters widened out and plunged deep even before the flood. Papa turned up there when the current slammed him against an outcropping of rock, pinning him briefly under the tree and breaking his arm and his ribs. Somehow, he managed to hold on to the rocks anyway and pulled himself most of the way out, though afterward he didn't recall that part very well.

Mary said that her dog must have heard Papa's groans down by the water's edge. The dog sat outside the door barking and howling until Mary finally stepped out to investigate. Straightaway she found Papa collapsed there in the frozen grass, one leg still dangling into the water. Mary threw her coat over Papa and helped him into the house where she laid out blankets for him in front of her fire. She pulled a fur hat down over his ears and tried to get some hot coffee into his cold stomach.

The dog curled up warm beside him.

As soon as Papa could move his lips enough to talk, he started babbling about how he had to find his little girl, but when he tried to stand up he keeled over backward and blacked out. When he came halfway back to his senses, he noticed the dog.

"Lewis and Clark?" he asked. The big black dog wagged its tail and licked his face.

"My dog's name is Jack," Mary told Papa. "He's my very best friend. He comes and goes all the time, but lucky for you he decided to stay home this week."

"But this is my little girl's dog," Papa protested weakly, "This is Lewis and Clark!"

Mary thought Papa was just delirious from exposure.

As it turned out though, it was Lewis and Clark. But on the other hand, it turned out that it was also Jack. Mary and I figured out later that we shared the same dog, or, as Mary put it, "This dog owns us both!" He must have been traveling the miles back and forth along the river from our house to hers for all those months. The great mystery of Lewis and Clark's wanderings was at last laid to rest.

Mary said that when she fished Papa from the river he looked like a rabbit that had been worked over twice in a laundry bucket and she knew he would never make it ten steps if he set out to find me, which he seemed determined to do. She promised him she would come get me instead, but she could hardly get a rough idea of where our house was before Papa fainted off again.

"Follow the dog," was the last thing Papa managed to tell her, "Just follow the dog." Mary heaped a pile of blankets over Papa, grabbed her lantern and a long rope, and hurried outside.

She tied her little boat behind her horse and followed Lewis and Clark straight up the waterline all those miles, pulling the boat behind like a sled over the icy ground. The whole time, she told me later, she thought she must be half crazy to be out in the cold following a silly dog on a wild-goose chase through the woods.

"For all I knew he was just out looking for rabbits!" she said.

But when our house was at last visible in the flood, Mary said that Lewis and Clark ran back and forth along the bank, whining frantically and looking for a way to cross, and she knew that he must have been there before and that this must be the place she was looking for.

The water curved in along a hill not far upriver. It was there that Mary lashed one end of her rope to a tree and pushed the boat out into the water, estimating that the current would carry her straight to me. Halfway out she could tell she was swinging wide of the house, so she reeled herself back in and tried launching from another tree further up the waterline. It took her three tries like that before she managed to reach me and bring me back to shore. That's why the boat had stopped and gone back the other way while Thaddeus and I were watching through the window that night.

The rest of the story about how Mary rescued me and took me back to my papa I've already told, except for one important thing that happened a few days later.

We were cleaning up from breakfast one day the next week, when Mary asked me out of the blue if I knew how to play the violin.

"I don't think I've ever even seen a violin," I said.

Mary looked a little puzzled. She finished scrubbing out a bowl and set it down.

"The other night," she said, "when I was floating out to your house in the flood, I thought I heard something that sounded like violins, but I couldn't tell where it was coming from. Do you remember hearing anything like that?"

I felt a big smile spreading across my whole face.

Mary had heard the angel music too.

CHAPTER 13

MARY RODE OUT EARLY to fetch the doctor the morning after she rescued us from the flood. The doctor showed up just before noon and splinted Papa up and gave him a bottle of whiskey to ease the sharp pains in his bones. He looked him over from head to toe and said it didn't look like there were any deeper injuries inside him, so apart from the broken bones and the blow to the head, all Papa had to show for his long ordeal was a mild frostbite and a nasty cold. After the doctor left, Papa slept for eighteen hours straight.

Faithful old Lewis and Clark hardly moved at all from Papa's side for three whole days until Papa started to stand up and move around some on his own.

"Lewis must be afraid that if he lets me out of his sight again I'll find myself some more trouble to get into," Papa said with a grin.

Papa and I ended up staying with Mary and Lewis and Clark for two whole weeks, almost up till Christmas. Mary cooked for us and tended to us that whole time. She and I took to staying up late almost every night too, talking and laughing and playing cards, and I finally did tell her all about Mama, but not till after we had known each other a week and had already decided to become best friends. Then Mary told me her mother had died too, but it happened when Mary was twenty-eight years old, not when she was just a baby. We were sad together when we talked that night, but the next day we both felt cheered up, like dark clouds had lifted from our hearts.

Word about mine and Papa's misfortune spread around by way of the doctor, and a few people that we knew, including Mr. Craven, came all the way out to Mary's to visit us.

I told Mr. Craven the story of how Thaddeus Frisco had helped save my life and I even included the part about the angel, but I'm sure Mr. Craven thought that part was my imagination on account of, as Papa once said, he wasn't one to ever put much stock in anything he hadn't seen for himself.

Mr. Craven responded saying he was sad that Thaddeus was gone, but as fate would have it, the good Lord had seen fit to show mercy on spiteful old Bartholomew. Bartholomew had wandered ashore on the opposite side of the river without washing more than a quarter mile down. An acquaintance of Mr. Craven's there had found him and put him up in a warm barn. The river was still too high for Mr. Craven to fetch him back, but he expected to within a week. "I never would have believed there'd come a day when I'd be happy to see that old mule," he laughed. Apparently, the good Lord still had some plans for Bartholomew.

CHAPTER 14

PAPA AND I WERE FORCED to take careful stock of our situation. In some ways, we hadn't fared nearly so well as Mr. Craven and his surviving mule. We had nowhere to live anymore, not even a warm barn. Our winter stores of food had disappeared along with our house and our clothes and our farm tools and our books and everything else we called our own, including three letters that Mama had written to Papa before they were married.

Mary would have gladly kept us through the winter at her place, but Papa couldn't bring himself to burden her indefinitely. Her house was even smaller than ours and her larder was only stocked for one person and besides, Papa said, it just wouldn't look right for an unmarried man and woman to live that long in the same house.

"Maybe you should get married then," I said, trying to be funny.

Mary laughed, but Papa's cheeks turned red. He stood up and walked out the door without saying a word.

That was when I first realized that Papa had grown a little bit fond of Mary too.

After that, I kept hoping that maybe Papa really would ask Mary to marry him so that we could all live together and become a family. But he never did. At least not back then right after the flood.

Later on a lot of things happened that none of us expected, but those are part of a whole different story that will have to wait for another telling. After all, as Papa likes to say, you can't ride two horses at one time.

With his slow-healing injuries making it so he wouldn't be fit to work again for several months, Papa finally decided that it would be best if he and I moved back East to live in Baltimore with his sister, at least for a while.

In all my seven years I had never been to Baltimore. I had never been anywhere, really, but the woods and the river and the fields around our house. We stayed on with Mary for three more days, and then she hitched up her horse, Fletcher, and took us on a carriage ride all the way into town where the train came through.

I thought I would never stop crying when I said good-bye to Mary, and I cried almost as hard saying good-bye to Lewis and Clark too, and Papa made Mary promise that if we sent her money she would buy a ticket and come to see us, and I made her promise that when she did she would bring Lewis and Clark with her, and then the conductor said "all aboard" and Papa and I had to step up into our train car and could only wave through the window as Mary and Lewis and Clark grew smaller and smaller walking along beside us while the train worked up steam.

"Write to us soon!" Mary yelled in a tiny voice that barely reached our ears from far away down the platform. Lewis and Clark gave one small bark before they receded from sight and were gone.

CHAPTER 15

I WAS SAD ENOUGH to cry as our train pulled away, but when I looked over at my papa, he seemed older and sadder than I had ever seen him. He looked thin and tired and cast down. Tears were spilling slowly from his eyes and running over his cheeks, and he didn't even raise his hand to wipe them away.

And I thought on it a while, until I understood why.

The last time Papa had ridden that train over those same tracks he'd been traveling the other way. He'd been a young man headed west with dreams of finding land and building a house and planting crops and raising a family. My mama would have been sitting proudly in the seat beside him.

Now, ten years later, he was leaving by those same tracks. And everything he had come here with, and everything he had worked so hard for afterward, was either gone, or dead, or washed away.

There was an old song that said something about slipping beneath the weight of broken dreams. I think that's what had happened to my papa.

He had come into our woods long ago with so many good things, and he had laid them all down there one by one. One by one he'd left them all behind and walked out empty-handed.

I was born to him in those same woods, and I was all that had passed through. I was all that had come out with him. For the first time in my life I saw that my papa was more than afraid. Almost losing me in the flood had broken his heart in some way that was hard to touch.

I put my hand on Papa's knee and smiled at him. He put his callused hand on top of mine and smiled back through the tears.

"We must be very brave, Papa," I told him as our train gathered speed, hurtling down the track toward Baltimore, "for the angel of the Lord goes before us."

Papa squeezed my hand and looked out the window at the hills that slowly rose and fell like the passing of days around us.

"You have known more angels in your young life than you can even count, Evangeline," he whispered softly.

Evangeline Elizabeth Blake. That's my given name.